KU-548-768

This Walker book belongs to:

_____

_____

_____

For Susan

First published 1999 by Walker Books Ltd
87 Vauxhall Walk, London SE11 5HJ

This edition published 2000

10 9 8 7 6 5

© 1999 Anita Jeram

The moral rights of the author/illustrator
have been asserted.

This book has been typeset in Kabel-Book Alt.

Printed in China

All rights reserved

British Library Cataloguing in Publication Data:
a catalogue record for this book
is available from the British Library.

ISBN: 978-0-7445-7283-4

www.walker.co.uk

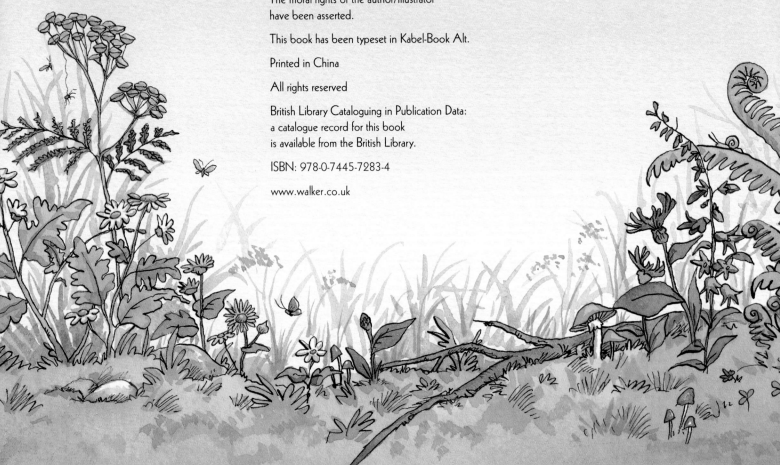

Bunny My Honey

Anita Jeram

WALKER BOOKS
AND SUBSIDIARIES
LONDON • BOSTON • SYDNEY • AUCKLAND

Mummy Rabbit had a baby.

His name was Bunny.

He looked just like his mummy,

only smaller.

He had long ears,

a twitchy nose and great big feet.

"Bunny, my Honey,"

Mummy Rabbit liked to call him.

Mummy Rabbit showed Bunny how to
do special rabbity things,

like running and hopping,

digging and twitching his nose

and thumping his great big feet.

Sometimes Bunny played with his best friends,
Little Duckling and Miss Mouse.
They played quack-quacky games,
squeaky games and thump-thump-thumpy games.

They sang,   We're the little Honeys.
A little Honey is sweet.
Quack quack, squeak squeak,
Thump your great big feet!

If a game ever ended in tears,

as games sometimes do,

Mummy Rabbit made it better.

"Don't cry, my little Honeys,"
Mummy Rabbit said. "I'm right here."

But one day Bunny got lost.

Oh, how could such a bad thing happen?

Perhaps it was a game that went wrong.

Perhaps Bunny ran too far on his own.

But there he was,
just one lost Bunny.

The more Bunny looked for

his friends and his mummy

the more lost

and the more lost

and the more lost he became.

Bunny started to cry.

"Mummy, Mummy,
I want my mummy!
Mummy, Mummy,
I want my mummy!"

"Bunny, my Honey!"

What was that?

"Bunny, my Honey!

Bunny, my Honey!"

"Bunny, my Honey!"

"MUMMY!"

Mummy Rabbit picked Bunny
up and cuddled him.

She stroked his long ears.

She put her twitchy nose
on his twitchy nose.

She kissed his great big feet.

Bunny's ears and nose
and feet felt warm all over.

"I love you, Mummy,"
Bunny whispered.
"I love you, Bunny, my Honey,"
Bunny's mummy
whispered back,
"and I love my other
little Honeys too."

On the way home, Bunny and
Miss Mouse and Little Duckling
sang their song.

We're the little Honeys.
A little Honey is sweet.
Quack quack, squeak squeak,
Thump your great big feet!

And Bunny was a
happy rabbit.

Another Little Honeys story

ISBN 978-0-7445-7857-7

Available from all good booksellers

www.walker.co.uk